THE
FROG PRINCE

by the
Brothers Grimm

Illustrated by
Robert Baxter

Troll Associates

Troll Associates, Mahwah, N.J.

Library of Congress Catalog Card Number: 78-18073
ISBN 0-89375-126-X

Long ago, when it was still worthwhile for people to wish for things, there was a king whose youngest daughter was very beautiful. Even the sun, which has seen everything in the world, seemed brightest when it shone on her face.

In a dark forest not too far from the king's palace, there was a deep well. The princess liked to sit in the shade near the well and play with her golden ball, tossing it into the air, and catching it when it came down. One day, the ball bounced right into the well. The princess watched helplessly as it sank down to the bottom. Then she began to cry, because the ball was her favorite toy.

Suddenly she heard a voice. "Why are you crying, princess?" The princess looked around, but all she saw was a big, ugly frog swimming in the well.

"Was that you?" she asked of the frog. "I'm crying because my golden ball fell into the well."

"Then cry no more," replied the frog. "I can get it for you. But in return, you must do something for me."

"Anything you ask," said the princess. "I will give you my pretty jewelry, my beautiful clothes, or even my golden crown."

"You don't understand," said the frog. "Your crown, your clothes, and your jewelry mean nothing to me. It is your friendship I want. Let me stay with you always, and be your playmate. When I am hungry, let me eat from your plate. When I am thirsty, let me drink from your cup. And when I am tired, let me sleep in your bed. Give me your promise, and I will fetch your golden ball from the bottom of the well.''

"I promise!" cried the princess, "I promise!" But as she watched the frog disappear deep into the well, she thought, "How silly! Who ever heard of a frog who can play with a princess! It's all so much nonsense!"

Soon the frog was back, holding the golden ball in his mouth. When he tossed it out of the well, the princess quickly picked it up and ran toward the castle.

"Wait for me!" croaked the frog. "You are running too fast! I cannot keep up with you!" But the princess did not listen, and soon the frog was far behind. Sadly, he turned around and hopped back to the well.

At dinnertime the next day, the princess was sitting next to her father, the king, when she heard something outside. *Plippety-ploppity*, up the castle stairs it came, and then there came a knock at the door. A voice cried out,

"Daughter of the king, come let me in!" The princess
went and opened the door. But as soon as she saw the
frog, she quickly shut it again, and went back to her place
at the table.

The king saw that she was afraid. "You look as if you have seen an ugly giant," he said. "Is that why you closed the door so quickly?"

"No, father," replied the princess. "It is not an ugly giant—it is an ugly frog. A horrid, dreadful frog." Then she told her father what the frog wanted. "Yesterday, my golden ball fell into the well. A frog heard me crying and said he would get it for me. But I had to promise that he could be my best friend. I never thought he would leave the water and follow me. But now he's at the door, and he wants to come in!"

Then everyone in the room heard the frog knocking
and crying out in a loud voice:
Oh princess, princess,
Listen to me.
Remember what
You promised to me?
Now open the door
And welcome me!

The king looked at his daughter and said, "A promise you give is a promise you must keep. Go now, and open the door."

As soon as the princess opened the door, the frog hopped into the room. He followed her to her place at the table and said, "I cannot reach. Lift me up onto your chair." The princess tried to pay no attention to him, but the king made her help the frog up. Still the frog could not reach, so he told the princess to help him onto the table.

"Your plate is too far away," croaked the frog.
"Bring it closer, so we can eat together." The princess
brought the golden plate closer. The very thought of
eating with a frog took her appetite away, but the frog ate
heartily.

Then the frog said, "My stomach is full, and I am growing tired. Please take me to your room, so I can sleep in your silken bed." At once, the princess began to cry. She did not want an ugly frog to sleep in her very own bed!

But the king was not moved by her tears. Instead, he became angry. "The promise you gave is the one you must keep!" he said firmly. "Do what your playmate asks."

So the princess picked up the frog and carried him upstairs to her bedroom. Ugh! How she hated to touch him! She set him down in a corner of the room and then she went to bed. Soon the frog came hopping over. "I am just as tired as you are," he croaked. "Let me sleep on your soft pillow. If you don't, I will have to tell your father!"

The princess became so angry that she hardly knew what she was doing. She reached down and grabbed the frog, crying, "You horrid creature! Go away and leave me alone!" Then she threw him against the wall.

At that very moment, a remarkable thing happened. Just as the frog struck the wall, he turned into a hand-some prince! He told the princess that a wicked witch had cast a spell on him and turned him into a frog. The princess was the only one who could have broken the spell.

And so it came to pass that the prince married the princess and took her to his father's kingdom, where they lived happily ever after.